Foreword

Two years ago, in the summer of 2020, with Covid-19 taking the world by storm, I created *Basketball Kid* out of my love for the game. At the time, I loved reading books by sports writer Mike Lupica. Similar to *Basketball Kid*, in Lupica's books, the main character is a kid who lives and breathes a sport like basketball or football. Then, a problem occurs (like losing a loved one or having a friendship issue), and the character uses the sport that they love as a way to help solve the problem. So in the boredom with the Covid Lockdown, I wanted to write a three to four-page story similar to Mike Lupica's writings as an activity. The short story kept growing as I included more detail as well as twists and turns to the plot. Before I knew it, it was over 70 pages, and I published the book with the title *Basketball Kid*. As for the inspiration behind the main character Erik Prent, I tried to create somebody I hoped the readers could connect to, so it feels like they are a part of the story.

Now, in the summer of 2022, at the age of 12, I am preparing for my Bar Mitzvah, a coming-of-age celebration celebrated for Jewish boys at the age of 13. An essential part of being a Bar Mitzvah is completing a mitzvah project, which is something that benefits your community in some way. One way to help a community is to raise money for a charity you care about. As I was thinking of ways to raise money, I felt like taking the profits from *Basketball Kid* would be a great way to benefit the community in two ways: raising money for a charity and giving people a book to read as an activity.

As a result, I realized I could use an extra two years of writing practice to improve *Basketball Kid*. I have created a new cover and back cover, made grammatical revisions, added more detail when necessary, and removed parts of the book that don't add anything to the plot. In addition, I have added chapters, page numbers, and additional scenes, including a funeral for Erik's father.

But most importantly, I will be donating 100% of the proceeds from the sales of this new edition of Basketball Kid to a charity I deeply care about- Children's Cancer Association. JoyRx, the mission delivery of Children's Cancer Association, brings Joy to young kids and teens with cancer and other serious illness by introducing them to new friends, or JoyRx Mentors, singing songs with them, and more.

Whether you have read the original *Basketball Kid* or not, I hope you enjoy this updated edition!

-Evan Goldstein

Chapter 1

"One more minute Erik!" my mom yelled from the kitchen.

Today was the day. It was finally going to be the eighth game of the basketball season after our two-week winter vacation. Although I was only 12 years old, I had big dreams of being the next star player in the NBA. I could already imagine my name, Eric Prent, on a giant statue one day in front of the Rose Garden in Portland, Oregon. My team's record was four wins and three losses, coming off a victory right before the break. "Coming!" I yelled back at her.

I put on my team's blue jersey, the same blue one I had worn all season. Our school didn't have much money, so we only had one color on our uniform. I proudly wore the number 24 after having scored 24 points in my very first basketball game at the age of nine.

As I walked through our rusty white door in our kitchen to leave, my dad whispered to me, "Good luck, kid. I'm really proud of you."

"Thanks, Dad," I whispered back to him.

My dad tried to come to all my games, but he was busy at work that day, so he couldn't attend. My nine-year-old brother Alex and I did our classical handshake; high-five, fist-bump, spin, spin, and then a chest bump to finish things. "See you later," my brother said.

Before all of my basketball games, I always got nervous. Being the star player on a team comes with a lot of weight on your shoulders, given that if you don't perform well, then it's not just you who has to deal with the consequences; it's those on your team. So when I got in the car, my legs immediately started trembling, and it was hard for me to talk without sounding like I was at the top of a cold and snowy mountain, my voice also trembling.

But for some reason, when I took a seat next to my mom on this very day, on top of the familiar nervous feelings for the game, I had a stomach ache and something that almost sounded like an alarm in my head. As she always was on the way to my games, my mom was quiet to "let me think through the game." So, to drown out the alarm-type noise in my head, I turned up the radio, and Jack Harlow's *First Class* got me pumped up for the game.

I felt a million times better when we arrived at the school gym. When we pulled out of our car, I smiled when I spotted my best friend, Leonard McCarthy.

"Wassup Leonard!" I instantly said.

"Are you ready for the big game today?" Leonard asked.

"You know I am!" I responded.

"See you in there," he concluded.

Although he was my best friend, some think Leonard looked atypical. He always had his black hair tied in a bun and had a significant scar on his forehead from slipping on spilled milk in the cafeteria in first grade.

That day we were playing against the Beaverton Blue Dogs. Last year, the Blue Dogs went to the semifinals in the Oregon Elite Youth

Basketball League, where they lost to the Portland Timberwolves, the same team that my team, the Hood River Ducks, failed to defeat in the quarter-finals last year.

As I opened the door to enter the gym, I knew that I had to focus and get locked in. "Aren't you pumped for the game?!" one of my teammates, Noah, yelled over to me over the cheering of another game somewhere else in the gym.

"Yes, I am!" I responded.

My mom took her seat in the front row of the middle section. "This is a big game we have here today, boys," Coach Modella announced during the pre-game huddle after our team did some stretching and layup lines. "Remember: Never get too high and never get too low," he continued. "Ducks on three!"

"One, two, three, Ducks!" our team yelled in unison.

The player I was guarding looked almost identical to me; blond, curly hair, around four foot eleven, and had long arms. The Blue Dogs wore white uniforms with a blue outline, much nicer than our jerseys.

"Good luck, dude," he whispered to me.

"Same to you," I responded.

From what I remembered from last year's game against the Blue Dogs, his name was Frederick. He was the star player on the Blue Dogs, and I knew I had to have a stellar defensive performance to stop him. That is when the ref began the game with a jump ball.

The game started slow for both teams. Each quarter was 12 minutes, so I wasn't worried. But by the end of the quarter, I did begin to worry as things were not going as planned. Frederick, the guy that I was guarding, well, supposed to be guarding, had 10 points in the game's first nine minutes. I, on the other hand, had yet to make a basket. The score was 17-3, the Blue Dogs on top. Our only points came when Noah hit a wide-open three-pointer on our fourth possession of the game. "This is unacceptable!" Coach Modella yelled at all of us.

"Erik! You have one job! Guard that little man!" he yelled at me.

"Sorry, coach," I uttered.

"I am taking you out for the rest of the half unless I say otherwise! You are letting the entire team and me down," Coach continued.

While Coach Modella is the nicest guy off the court, on the court, all he wants to do is win. Does he make me a better player? Absolutely. Does he know what the word "fun" is? Absolutely not. "Don't let it get to you. Just brush it off," Leonard said, trying to encourage me as he put his arm around my shoulders.

I just shrugged and looked for my mom. She wasn't there. Maybe she had a call with her boss or something. I just tried to ignore what was happening off the court and stay in the game, maybe try to find some patterns in the Blue Dogs' play style.

The start of the second quarter was not much different than the first. Frederick had another eight points while the rest of his team scored five. The only points my team had were when Leonard had a sweet backdoor pass to Antonio, another great player on my team, and he made the easy layup. The score was 30-5.

I loved everybody on my team. All of them were super kind to me, except for one player. His name was Gary Anderson. He wasn't just mean to me but to everybody on the Ducks. The good thing was that Coach Modella noticed these mean actions, and he barely put him in. The only chance he had to play more than 5 minutes a game was if Leonard got hurt or was in foul trouble.

"You're trash, bobblehead," Gary whispered to me.

"Thanks," I responded to him, just trying to ignore him.

He said something under his breath, but I couldn't make it out.

"Erik! You are back in the game!" I heard Coach say.

This was my moment. I looked up in the stands to look for my mom. I caught a glimpse of her running to the restroom, tears streaming down her face. Something was wrong.

As I got back onto the court, all of my worries somehow disappeared. That was the beauty of basketball. This was my time to show everybody how good of a player I truly am.

My team's first possession was an absolute mess. Lukas, another kid on my team, inbounded the ball to Leonard. Leonard was one of those kids that were kind of a show-off. He, unfortunately, decided to do a behind-the-back pass. It fell right into the hands of Frederick. He scooped it up and pulled up for a three. Nothing but net. 33-5.

I knew I had to flip the switch with the game getting out of hand. That's when I started getting hot. Really hot. Lukas inbounded the ball to Leonard, who made a great bounce pass to me after faking the chest pass, making the defender look like he was jumping on a trampoline. "Here! Erik, here!" I heard three people on my team scream.

I looked Leonard straight in the eye. Frederick, still guarding me, went to where Leonard was, leaving me wide open. I took a dribble to the left and pulled up for the three-pointer. The ball took a soft bounce from the left side of the rim and into the hoop. Bucket!

Two plays later, I completely juked out a defender with a double crossover, leaving him in the dust, and went in for the easy layup. By halftime, I had 17 points, and we were back in the game, only down by 8 points as Antonio had Frederick locked down (towards the end of the quarter, Coach wanted to give me a break from guarding Frederick and gave Antonio the honors). The score was 38-30.

At halftime, just as I walked to the end of the bench to grab my water bottle, my mom came down from the bleachers, eyes still filled with tears. "Erik. Come over here. I have to tell you something," my mom cried.

I walked over to her, a little confused but sensing something was seriously wrong. "It's your dad."

"What about dad?" I whispered to her.

"I just heard from his boss that he died in a fire at work," my mom

cried even louder this time.

Chapter 2

I couldn't believe it. I looked over at my team. The first person I saw was Gary, who had half a smile. You would think even the meanest people would have a little compassion for those who lost a loved one. Obviously not. I was so mad at Gary but didn't have the strength to say anything.

"Your father was a hero today," my mom whispered. "He saved his boss's life by running into the fire and getting him out of the office safely. But it was too late for him."

Tears started gushing out of my eyes, making a huge puddle on the court. This was the worst day of my life.

That night I sat in my bed, crying. I had never dealt with a tragedy like this before. I had no idea how to deal with, or even comprehend, what had just happened. I had just lost my father.

I left the game at halftime. Shortly after the game's final buzzer, Leonard had texted me saying we lost 59-48. He couldn't say a word when I explained why I had left early.

For the first time in my life, I didn't care what the score was. I turned off my phone, only being able to think about one thing and one thing only: My dad. I tried to close my eyes and get some rest, but it was next to impossible. I tried listening to *The Dan Patrick Show* to help me fall asleep, but I still couldn't. For hours I tossed and turned, images of my dad popping up in my head nonstop.

I woke up the next morning feeling sick to my stomach. I didn't go to school, and I didn't go to basketball practice. I spent most of the day in my room looking at pictures of my dad. He was a great man. I was proud to be his son. I still was in disbelief.

After practice, Leonard came over. We didn't talk much, but we still played some basketball. I beat him in two of the three games we played, which made me feel better. We played our hearts out during the game, scoring every chance we got.

Right before Leonard left, he said something very meaningful to me. "I know you don't want to talk about it, but listen. I'm sure that if your dad were here, he would tell you that you need to continue doing what makes you feel better: playing basketball. You have to continue, or else you will be like this for the rest of your life," Leonard said, a tear or two streaming down his cheek.

"Thank you for always being here for me," I said to Leonard.

With that, Leonard left. He was right. My dad would not want me just crying all day. He would want me to do what makes me happy. I knew I would go to school and basketball practice the next day.

The next morning, as I was getting ready for school, I felt like something was missing. I didn't know until I sat in the car. It was the feeling that my dad would not always be there for me. One of my favorite parts of the day was coming home from school and talking sports with my dad. It was hard to wrap my mind around the idea that he wouldn't be there.

When I arrived at school, everybody grew very quiet. They had obviously heard the news about what happened to my dad, given that typically everybody would crowd around me and talk about who had the best basketball and football cards. That day was different. I just walked to my locker, grabbed my stuff, and continued walking to my first class, which was math.

We had to take a pop quiz about dividing, multiplying, adding, and subtracting fractions. Luckily, I got 97% of the questions on the quiz correct. "I would like to give a special shout-out to Erik. You scored the best on this quiz, and for that, I will give you two stickers!" my math teacher Mrs. Kentsborne exclaimed.

My teacher had this cool little thing where you earned an extra ten minutes of recess if you got five stickers.

I wasn't the type of person that bragged a lot, so I just sat at my desk and said, "Thank you, Mrs. Kentsborne," trying not to make any eye contact given that my face was still red from crying.

Inside my head, I gave myself a fist bump because the girl I had liked for the past year, Rachel Tarensky, smiled at me. Maybe going to school wasn't such a bad idea. Until lunch.

As I sat down for lunch next to Leonard, I saw Gary come towards us. "Fancy to see you annoying little kids here," Gary announced as he sat down.

"Just so you know Gary, you are at least half-a-foot shorter than me, so don't say that we are "little kids" ever again," Leonard acknowledged, almost laughing.

Gary's face turned so red that it almost made me laugh, something I had not done since hearing about my dad's passing. "I am the king of the world, and you are not!" Gary half-yelled.

"Sorry, but that just sounded dumb. You are making no sense today. You better go to a joke teacher," Leonard added.

Gary was so mad that he walked away for the first time in at least three months. "You are a legend, Leonard," I said.

"That is what happens when you are the best player on your basketball team," Leonard whispered so only I could hear.

"Now you are the one that needs to go to the joke teacher," I joked.

"I appreciate it," he concluded.

Just when I thought lunch would be the best ever, at least given that I was dealing with the worst trauma of my life, things went south. Just as we left the cafeteria, Leonard decided to say one last word to Gary. "See you at joke school, Gary."

With that, Gary kicked him as hard as he could in the shins. Leonard immediately fell to the ground screaming. "You are a jerk!" Leonard yelled at Gary.

My Science teacher Mr. Teradura and I helped Leonard up and immediately took him to the doctor's office. As we were going up the stairs, I heard one of the seventh graders saying that Gary would for sure be suspended from school, but I didn't have room in my cramped-up little head to think about that. I could only think about the worst-case scenario for Leonard. Could he be done for the season?

Once we finally arrived at the Hood River Public School's doctor's office, the nurse immediately called Leonard's mom Rebecca. "I believe we have a serious situation with your son Leonard," I heard the nurse say to Leonard's mom.

I couldn't hear the rest of the conversation except for something about going to a hospital immediately.

"I hope you feel better," I said to Leonard as he was going to the ambulance where he was supposed to meet his mom.

That night, I could barely sleep. I just sat in my bed and waited for
Leonard to text me. My phone's text message ringtone sounded,
meaning someone had texted me.

That someone ended up being Leonard. "i am out 4 the rest of the
season unless we make it 2 the finals."

Chapter 3

How could he have gotten kicked in the shins, and now he's out for the entire season? I hoped it was a joke and he would tell me the truth, but after at least 5 minutes, he didn't text me.

I decided to play NBA 2K on the Xbox I got for my birthday last year. I tried not to think of the one who gave me the awesome gift, as it would just make me tear up all over again, and I knew he wouldn't want me to be sad. My team was the Trail Blazers because I lived right near Portland. I played until my mom told me in a loud screeching voice that it was past my bedtime.

The following morning I woke up in a bad mood, even though it was Friday and I had two basketball games this weekend. This was a big thing because there were only 11 games in the regular season. "Are you ready for breakfast, honey?" I heard my mom yell while I was getting dressed.

"I am coming right this second," I responded.

Just as I sat down for breakfast, I started to cry. When I say cry, I mean huge drops of tears. "Erik, Erik, no, don't cry. We're all in this together. Please don't cry. It just makes me sad to see you cry about him. It's hard on everyone, honey. But we'll get past this," my mom said, trying to keep her calm and not start balling out in tears.

Even though I wanted to yell at her, and that I wouldn't get past this obstacle, I knew deep down inside that she was hurting just as much as me, if not more. That made me, as my mom had said, feel supported and I had loved ones around me.

While I was sad about the loss of my father, I still had my mom to support me and help me get through the loss. My mom, on the other hand, didn't really have anybody who she could go to. That was when I felt *really* bad for her.

While I was focused on myself and how nobody in the world could be having it worse than me, my mom also was suffering. She had known my dad for nearly twice as long as I had known him, yet she tried to not show her sadness because she had to be there for Alex and me.

I gave her a hug, knowing that she needed it. Even though I couldn't help her get through it like she was for me, all I could do was try my best, and that all starts with her knowing she is loved.

On my walk up to school, all I could think about was how strong she was for hiding her emotions and making sure that we would get through the tough times. When I arrived at school, I instantly ran over to Leonard, who had crutches with him. Excluding my mom, he was the only person that could make me feel happy these days. "How are you feeling?" I instantly said to him.

Although I had cried a few seconds earlier, I did my best to hide it because I genuinely felt bad for him. My other friends Liam and Cooper gathered around him, asking questions. "When will you be better? How are you feeling? How did your mom react when she saw you?" we all questioned.

"I can talk later. I have to get Social Studies in ten minutes, and I don't want to be late!" he said, words rushing out of his mouth like water running over a waterfall.

"If it starts in ten minutes and it will take at most twenty seconds to get there, then what is the rush?" Liam asked.

"There is no such thing as being too early," Leonard said with a huge smile.

"You sound like a legit wizard when you talk like that," I added.

"See you guys around," Leonard said.

The day was much calmer without Gary, having been suspended for three weeks. I felt much better knowing I wouldn't have anybody trying to bring me down nonstop.

Leonard still attended basketball practice, being our official assistant coach. "That was a great play you just ran there, Erik," Leonard said during practice after I had set a screen for Antonio and then cut to the corner for a fadeaway three that rattled in.

"Thanks!" I responded.

Now that practice was practically over, we all huddled in a small group. "We have a situation. Leonard is out injured, and Gary is suspended for three weeks. We need somebody to be our point guard," Coach said in the huddle.

I did not volunteer because my dream was to be the next Michael Jordan, who was a shooting guard, not a point guard. Nobody on my team raised their hand, knowing that being a point guard comes with a lot of pressure. "Our team's new point guard is… Erik!" Coach Modella announced in an enthusiastic voice.

Chapter 4

I could not believe it. Those seven words just crushed my dreams of being the next Michael Jordan.

"You will be starting tomorrow. I hope that you don't let this team down."

"Be honest. Is this a big step up or down for you?" Leonard asked as we left the huddle.

"Definitely a step down because I have always wanted to be the next Michael Jordan, who was a shooting guard. And I also really liked playing the two," I responded sorrowfully.

"I know, but think about it: Dame. Curry. Doncic. Ice Trae. All of your favorite players to watch right now. They're all point guards!" Leonard added.

"I guess you're right. See you at the game tomorrow," I said to Leonard as he crutched out of the building.

He was obviously in a hurry because he didn't respond. "Thank you, Coach," I said to Coach Modella as he packed up all the basketballs and cones.

"You're welcome, Erik. Again, I am truly sorry about what happened to your father. Is there anything I can do to help?" Coach asked.

"Thank you, but for now, not really. Can you give me some tips for being a great point guard?" I asked.

"Erik, we're waiting for you!" my mom yelled from the door to leave the old basketball gym.

"Can we talk about this tomorrow before the game if we have time? My mom gets picky when her food gets cold," I added.

He chuckled and nodded his head. The car ride was very silent, with nobody talking except when Alex bragged about how he aced his math quiz. Ever since my father died, things had been way worse.

Chapter 5

The next morning, I woke up very excited. It was game day! "Time to go, honey!" my mom yelled from downstairs.

For some reason, my mom always had to yell. Even last night at dinner, she was loud. I was about two feet away from her, and she just screamed as loud as she could regarding my napkin not being on my lap. I have no idea why she yells. It's probably because of dad. I knew that the funeral that was taking place a couple of hours after the game would be emotional. My mom asked if I could make a one-minute speech, which I had just finished writing.

I got in our black Volvo and started reading my book about point guards. I thought it might contain tips about being a great point guard. Since it didn't have the information I was looking for, I was about to ask my dad until I realized he wasn't there to answer my questions. It really did suck.

I finally entered the gym. Nobody was there to accompany me, so I just sprinted inside. I got there a little late, so Coach Modella had no time to help me figure out my new position. I ran onto the court, shook hands with the guy I was guarding, and started playing. The opposing team wore orange and green outfits, which I thought looked pretty cool.

My team's odds of winning this game were slim because the team we were playing, the Portland Timberwolves, was the best in the league. Their star player, Alfonzo Robertson, scored 42 points in their last game, and their team scored 64. This Alfonzo kid was a beast.

The second the ball was tipped, all the sadness I had felt about my father's passing disappeared. Of course, I was still sad about what had happened, but once the whistle was blown and the referee threw the ball in the air, I could just focus on the game and leave everything else behind me. That was when I realized that basketball was my escape. Playing ball has always helped me feel better when anything terrible happened to me. And especially in the most challenging times like losing a loved one, I felt basketball can help get past it.

My team won the jump ball, and I suddenly had the ball in my hands. After four dribbles, I saw Antonio cut right under the hoop. I made a one-handed bounce pass, and he scored the easy layup. "That's what I'm talking about!" Coach Modella exclaimed from our bench.

Alfonzo responded on a layup of his own, driving to the hoop without looking up to pass the rock. It went back and forth until the second quarter began. The score was 19-16, our team winning, but not by much. It took me a moment to realize that I did all that while being a point guard. Maybe Leonard was right.

To start the second quarter, I felt Coach made the mistake of not putting me in. The first few possessions were fine, my team converting two out of three shots, both of which were layups. The other team converted their first three shots, all of which were either layups or floaters from the elbow made by Alfonzo.

That's when things started to fall apart. Antonio couldn't hit the buckets we needed inside the paint, nor could Bodhi, another player on my team, around the arc. The Wolves, on the other hand, went on a run. This one brown-haired kid with freckles, a great three-point shooter on their team, converted four out of five shots from beyond the arc. Our only other bucket in the quarter was when Bodhi completely juked out the defender, clearing space for him to shoot a three-ball, and converted. By the end of the half, the score was 38-26. "I can't believe it! You guys couldn't make anything that quarter, except for two layups and one lucky three-pointer," Coach said in the halftime huddle.

"That was not luck. That was all skill," Bodhi interjected.

"Doesn't matter. Either way, that quarter was terrible. This quarter, we will be giving the ball only to Erik unless somebody else has a wide-open shot," Coach Modella continued.

"Now, let's get this second half back!" Coach Modella concluded.

I got back out there, all fired up and ready to go. I dribbled the ball up to the three-point line on my team's first possession. Everybody on the opposing team knew I only tried to go for layups. But I proved them wrong by nailing my first three-point attempt of the game, doing what Steph Curry does on TV where he turns around before it even goes in, knowing that it was gold. The Timberwolves failed to respond. Alfonzo missed another easy layup that he should have converted. Antonio got the rebound and threw the ball upcourt quarterback style as far as he could. The ball landed just a step in front of me, and I took the easy layup off the backboard.

Just like that, we scored five points in less than a minute. "We can win this game," I whispered to Noah, a great player on my team.

"We *will* win this game," he responded, eyes still wholly glued to the basketball.

Alfonzo dribbled the ball up, eyes fixed on the brown-haired kid who couldn't miss from range. I noticed on the bench that Alfonzo always looked to who he would pass the ball. Just as the ball left his hands on its way to the intended target, I charged through, intercepting the ball and started heading upcourt. Bodhi took a nice line towards the hoop, so I passed him the rock. The ball landed one foot in front of Bodhi. He grabbed the ball and took the easy layup but missed what seemed like an easy two points. Luckily, Antonio was right under the hoop. He grabbed the rebound but also missed the put-back shot off the glass. I grabbed the rebound, did a pump fake, saw the brown-haired kid jump toward me, absorbed the contact, and nailed the two-foot shot, getting fouled by the kid with freckles (I think his name was Terry because his coach yelled at him after fouling me) in the process.

I sank the free throw, hitting only net, and got back on defense. A three-point play! "That was like a circus! No more missing two shots in two seconds!" Coach yelled from the sidelines.

After the free throw, my team only scored five more points, two scored by me and three by Antonio. However, the Timberwolves weren't lighting up the scoreboard either. By the end of the quarter, the score was close at 36-32. "This is why we are known as one of the best teams in Oregon! Because we come together as a team when it matters most!" Coach Modella exclaimed.

"Thank you, Coach!" I heard Noah say from behind me.

"Leonard, I want you to lead the team in the chant! Ducks on three!

"One, two, three, Ducks!" Leonard led the team in chanting.

Coach sat me for the first four minutes of the quarter, which I supported because that gave me time to rest. While on the bench, I watched the Timberwolves' passing, shooting, and dribbling patterns intently. Over three minutes, I noticed three observations: Terry always dribbled once to the left before shooting, Alfonzo only passed to Terry or this other guy whose name was either Kevin or Devin, and the inbounds pass always went to Terry or Alfonzo.

By the time I entered the game, the Timberwolves had put on a little comeback and had a lead of three, 44-41, with nine minutes remaining. When I stepped foot onto the court, I knew there was no way that I was coming off until the buzzer sounded (unless I got injured), so inside of my head, I promised myself to win the game for my dad. Terry inbounded the ball to Alfonzo (just like I noticed while watching from the bench), and he dribbled about twenty feet before taking a shot from the elbow. This time, not only did Alfonzo make the shot, he hit nothing but net, which is a noise that I hear a lot as a basketball player. The crowd, filled with parents and friends, cheered after the made basket.

When we got the ball back, most of the other players on the Timberwolves were still celebrating, so when Antonio inbounded the ball to me, I was wide open at the three-point line. I took the shot, missed it just short, got my own rebound, and flipped a no-looker to Noah, who nailed the three-pointer in the corner. "Somebody finally missed a shot!" I heard Leonard joking from the sidelines.

I did manage to chuckle, then got right back into the game. It went like that for the next seven-and-a-half minutes of play. Alfonzo would make a layup, and my team would respond, nailing a three-pointer or mid-range shot. Not a lot of defense was being played.

My coach called timeout with 20 seconds left in the game. The score was 61-60, our team winning. I could hear the other team's coach screaming at the players, an interesting scene. All Coach Modella could say was, "Play hard defense. Guard your man. We'll likely have one final chance to win if they make a shot. We can do this!"

The lineup to end the game was the same five players we started with: Antonio, Bodhi, Noah, Adam, and I. This was it. If we lost this game, we were *extremely* likely to be out of the final four tournament unless the teams ahead of us could lose out and we could handle our business.

Alfonzo inbounded the ball to Kevin (I confirmed that it was Kevin when the Timberwolves coach called out his name while in the huddle), who instantly passed the ball to Terry. He took the three-pointer but missed it short! Unfortunately, Mark, a player for the Timberwolves, was right under the hoop, and he passed it right back to Terry at the three-point line. Ten seconds. Terry did a pump fake, drawing Antonio, a very tall and smart player, away from Alfonzo. Seeing his teammate open, Terry passed the ball to Alfonzo, who was open for three. Seven seconds. Alfonzo took the shot. The gym became very quiet as the ball was in the air. Nothing but net.

The small crowd went wild, a few kids even jumping on the bleachers. We called our last time out. Four seconds left in the game. 63-61, the Timberwolves on top. We all gathered in the huddle listening to our coach. "We have the ball at the baseline. By the time we inbound it, we will have about three seconds to shoot it. Our best chance at making a deep three is with Erik. Let's try to get him the ball, and hope he can get up the court quick enough to get a shot off in his range," Coach said.

"All of the pressure is on you, Erik!" Leonard half-joked.

"Thank you. That helps a lot," I joked back to him.

Our team's best passer was Antonio, so he was the inbounder. I was right where I was supposed to be. Everything was going just as planned. Until Antonio made the mistake of looking straight at me. Just as he passed me the ball, Alfonzo intercepted it and dribbled the game out. Ball game. We lost. Again.

Chapter 6

Bodhi's mom was the snack person, but nobody had much of an appetite because we had just lost our second straight game of the season, and we were probably out of the playoffs. "We have another game tomorrow!" Leonard exclaimed, trying to cheer everyone up.

The saddest person on the team was Antonio, who had made the bad pass at the end. He was crying, tears streaming down his cheeks. Just moments before, he was all excited and energetic, and now he was crying. "It's not your fault Antonio. Basketball is a team sport. We all could have done something better to win. We didn't, and that is fine," I said, trying to sound happy.

"Thank you, Erik," he said as he looked up, trying to break a smile.

I walked away to give him some space and ran to where my mom was. "You played great, honey!" she exclaimed.

"Thank you, mom," I said, although I was sad because my team had made the playoffs in the two years I had played ball, and it seemed like this year would be different.

For some reason, my mom had to embarrass me in front of everybody in the gym, yelling, "Good job, Ducks!"

The car ride home was quiet, leaving me to read my book in complete silence. "Do you think we will win at least once more before the season's over? We played decent the entire season until winter break, and now we are terrible. Are we ever going to be good again?" I asked my mom as we were sitting in the car.

"It depends on how you guys play. If you guys play like you did today, I am sure of it," she said as if she believed what she was saying.

There were 12 teams in our league, and we were currently in 8th place. The top four make it to the playoffs. We had little chance at this point of making it.

"Now go change into the clothes I have laid out for you," my mom said once we finally pulled into our driveway.

I had no idea what she was talking about for a second until I remembered that the funeral was soon. I ran to my room and put on the white button-down and the black suit my mom had laid out. I read over my speech one more time, then ran back downstairs. After we ate lunch, my mom, Alex, and I drove to the cemetery where my dad would be buried.

We were the first ones there, and throughout half an hour, friends and family started to arrive, all of them offering their condolences. They would share the stories they had with my dad, which made me realize how amazing of a man my father was. The ceremony was beautiful, and it took everything I had to keep my composure and not start crying. Then, it was my turn to speak.

I went up to where the funeral leader had been, lowered the microphone slightly, and began reading what I had written. "Thank you all for being here today to honor my dad. I know that he would be so grateful for all who are in attendance today. My dad was a–" I began, then cut myself off.

Even though I was super proud of the speech I had written, unlimited words and stories showed how amazing my dad was, and what I had written didn't even begin to show how much I loved him. I stopped reading what I had written and looked out at the 25 or so people in attendance and began to just speak from the heart, something my dad had always taught me to do. "My dad was such an amazing man. It is horrible even to think that he had to pass away at such a young age, especially for a man that still had such a great life ahead of him. Even the smallest things   that he would do for me I appreciate so much. I still remember when I tried out for a basketball team for the first time when I was nine years old, there was the A team and the B team. The coaches tried to convince us that the teams were equal, but we all knew otherwise. I did not make the A team and got placed on the B team, and my dad noticed I was upset," I continued.

Just thinking of the memory, I started crying, but I continued. "There was a week before the season started, so my dad practiced with me nonstop for a week so I could improve on my game. He improved my form, told me to bend my knees more when I shot, and got me to be a better left-handed dribbler. He had meetings and work to do. He was a busy man. But for that week, the second I came back from school, we would go into our driveway to work on my basketball skills. Fast forward to the season's first game, I scored 24 points, and our team won 28-23. At the next practice, the A-team coach told me that I was being moved up to his team. If it wasn't for my dad, that never happens, and I honestly don't think I would care as much about basketball as I do now. He was always looking out for others, trying to bring a smile to the faces of those around him."

At this point, I was full-on crying, and I doubted anyone in attendance could understand what I was saying. I knew I had been speaking for over a minute, so I wrapped things up with, "As I said before, my dad was such a great man, and it is awful that he died at such a young age, but it has gotten me to appreciate life so much more. Thank you."

Chapter 7

Many people there were crying, though my eyes were so blurry I couldn't tell. Afterward, people walked up to me and said it was a beautiful speech. It made me feel good. For some time after the ceremony was over, people started sharing more of their stories, and when we finally got home, it was almost time for dinner.

I told my mom I would shoot around until it was time to eat. I went inside our garage and brought out our Spalding basketball hoop. I hadn't used it since my father died, so it was a bit rusty. When I was a little kid, I always played basketball in our driveway, but now I hardly used the hoop because I played basketball every day at recess and basketball practice almost every day of the week.

I started doing the drills that I did with my dad in that week leading up to my first basketball season that I talked about in my speech, but at a more advanced level. I started doing simple layups, lefty and righty, and slowly started moving back until I was draining deep threes. I had shot around for probably 30 minutes when my mom said, "It's time for dinner!"

Alex instantly ran to the dinner table, and I responded, "I'll skip dinner! I'm not that hungry anyway!"

My mom did not argue with me. Although I was hungry, I didn't say so. I was getting a lot better, and I didn't want to have to stop now. I played until it got really dark. When I was about to enter the house, I heard a voice. I recognized that voice. That voice belonged to my father. "Remember what I told you about bending your knees," I heard him say.

That was it! The reason why we weren't converting on our shots was that we weren't bending our knees! I talked about it during my speech but was so emotional that I didn't think about what I was saying. Although I knew my father wasn't actually there, I could hear him talking in my head. I needed to get to the game early to remind everyone on my team to bend their knees more when they shoot!

I turned on the lights to see the hoop and started shooting. With the trick of bending my knees, I made nine of my last ten buckets. It was incredible how just one trick changed my entire outlook.

That night I decided not to tell anyone how late I stayed up to play basketball. I had to wake up at 8:00 a.m. for my basketball game at 9:00 a.m. Remembering everything my dad had ever told me about basketball and knowing that my funeral speech had moved many, I went to sleep like a true champ.

I woke up the following morning feeling awesome. I looked over at the clock and saw that it was 8:15 a.m. I had to leave immediately! I woke up my mom, who was still sleeping, and at first, it looked like she would never wake up. "I have to get to my game today!" I told her as she finally woke up.

"Do you want eggs and cereal for breakfast?" she asked.

"I don't need breakfast! Can we just get in the car already?" I said back to her in a rush.

"What's the rush?" she questioned, eyes still very sleepy from the night before.

"I'll explain when we are in the car! Bring Alex in the car and call it good," I responded, still in a rush to get to the gym.

As we were in the car, I felt like the whole world was mad at me. Alex was screaming at me for waking him up, and mom was yelling even louder than usual about why I was in such a rush.

"I'm in a rush because I remembered something that dad had once told me. It's the reason why we aren't winning games. We aren't bending our knees!" I exclaimed, thinking that they might know what I was talking about.

My mom was clueless because she responded, "Of course, that can help you guys on defense!"

We finally arrived at the gym, which took about 40 minutes from Hood River, as it was a road game in Troutdale. I ran inside the gym, leaving my brother and mom sitting in the car, not knowing what to do.

When I finally entered the gym, I spotted my coach giving out positions. "Coach Modella! Wait!" I yelled from across the court.

"What is it, Erik? We don't have much time for your jokes," he said.

"It's not a joke! We aren't winning games because we are not bending our knees," I said in a rush.

He didn't say anything, but he nodded and smiled, showing that he was waiting for one of us to say that. "That is true. Especially since our team has some great shooters, we like to take deep shots, and the only way to make those is by bending your knees more," Coach said with a big smile still stuck to his face.

The Troutdale Chargers wore their yellow outfits, which were super nice and probably expensive too. As our starters took the court, I heard Leonard yell, "Let's go, Ducks!" with a big grin.

The Chargers won the jump ball, and their star player Terrance Kataro started dribbling up the court. He passed to another Chargers player named Phil, who took the shot. It hit the backboard and landed in the hands of Adam.

Adam passed to me, and I dribbled up the court. When I was around the three-point line, I gave Antonio the signal to set a screen for me. He did, leaving me the opening to shoot the three-ball. I bent my knees a little more than I had previously and made it, bringing a "Wow" to the crowd.

Terrance got the inbounds pass right where he needed it, giving him the perfect opening to nail the layup. The only way they scored for the whole quarter was with Terrance converting on layups, which he only did three times in twelve minutes. All of our starters scored at least four points. It was our best quarter of the season!

Our best basket was when Bodhi drew the defender to the left, dribbled through the defender's legs, and made a layup. The defender who had gotten juked ran to the sidelines to ask the coach to be benched. It was hysterical.

By the end of the quarter, we were winning 28-6. "This is how Hood River basketball is supposed to be played!" Coach Modella exclaimed.

"If we continue to make shots like we are right now, we have a good chance of sending these folks home without a win," Coach added.

He sent all of the second-string players in for the whole second quarter. Jack, the best of the backup players, was the point guard. He did a great job replacing me, making two of two shots. I had no idea why he wasn't a starter, being our second-best shooter, but I didn't want to talk to Coach about something that had nothing to do with me.

The rest of the second unit also played great. On one of the plays, Sam, who joined our team after the 2nd game of the season, set a sweet screen for Jack to convert on a fadeaway three-pointer.

The Chargers, on the other hand, could still not make anything. Their only bucket was when Terrance set a screen for Phil, who got the easy layup. The score at the end of the half was 47-8.

"We are playing great this first half! This may be the best first half of basketball I have seen in my coaching career!" he exclaimed.

Coach Modella continued playing the backup players, even though the starters always played in the third quarter. Our team started with the ball. Jack inbounded the ball to Michael, a player for the Ducks, who dribbled up the court with the ball. He passed the ball back to Jack, who then had a nice bounce pass to Sam who cut under the hoop and hit a reverse layup.

The Chargers noticeably had a good pep talk at halftime because out of the gate, their players started playing like they wanted to win the game. On their first possession of the second half, Terrance got the ball and passed it to Josh, a player for the Chargers, who was standing at the three-point line with nobody guarding him. The second he received the ball, he shot it. Splash.

When Jack got the inbound pass, Terrance stole it and got the floater with Jack on his tail. "What was that sloppiness about?" Coach yelled at all of the players on the court.

We responded when Jack made a three-pointer off of the assist from Michael. After the three-ball, nobody made any of the shots except for a three made by Terrance.

At the end of the quarter, the score was 53-16, the Ducks winning.

I wondered if Coach Modella was going to put the starters in for the final quarter. In the huddle, Coach explained his decision. "If we put the starters in, there is a chance that one of them will get injured, which is something that we can't afford. Since there is the policy that starters must play at least 18 minutes per game, I will put the starters in for half of the fourth quarter," Coach explained.

"Let's finish this game off strong!" Coach Modella concluded.

As I took the court, I may have gotten a little too excited about winning our first game in a while that I tripped over my laces. It was pretty embarrassing.

When Antonio passed the ball to me, I got nervous because Terrance was approaching me with a lot of speed. Right as the ball reached my hands, I tried to tuck it away, but it was too late. Terrance grabbed it from me, but when he finally got the rock, he took one dribble, and it bounced off the side of his shoe, heading out of bounds. Terrance, Antonio, and I all jumped out for the ball at once. I was the first to go for the ball, and Antonio and Terrance painfully dogpiled on top of me. I heard the referee blowing his whistle, so I shuffled my way out of the dogpile and to where Terrance was standing.

However, Antonio was still on the floor, reaching for his ankle. He had gotten hurt. Coach immediately ran over. I heard Coach ask Antonio a few questions, but the only response I heard was, "I can't play for the rest of the game."

I could not believe it. First, Leonard got hurt, and now Antonio was injured.

Adam's dad, who happened to be a doctor, ran onto the court to try to see if Antonio was okay, and after about a minute, I heard him say, "Antonio, as much as I hate to say this, you may be done for the rest of the year."

Chapter 8

That was followed by loud crying. Who would replace Antonio at the center position? *Was* he replaceable? There were a lot of unanswered questions.

When Antonio was off the court, Coach still let the starters play for six more minutes. I was guessing that our team would be terrible without Antonio. His backup would be Sam, who wasn't a bad player, but would never be as good as Antonio.

Without Antonio, our team did indeed struggle. In the six minutes that we played, we scored only three points. The Troutdale Chargers, on the other hand, played great. Terrance went on a run, making three of four shots from beyond the arc, and he converted four out of four shots inside the three-point line, most of which were his floaters that were automatic. The rest of his team also played well, racking up seven points. The Chargers had scored 24 points in six minutes. Halfway through the quarter, we were still winning 56-40.

Coach made the subs, taking out all the starters and putting in the backups, including Sam. "Finish this game off for us!" Coach shouted out to all the players for the Ducks on the court.

The other team's coach took Terrance out, meaning they probably knew the game was out of reach. The rest of the game became about dribbling and passing the ball, trying to run out the clock. Only one shot was taken when Sam tried to make a three-point buzzer-beater. Disappointingly, he air-balled it, which I found pretty funny.

Although we had won our first game since winter break, nobody was excited. "At least we won the game," Bodhi said, though in a dejected voice.

In the huddle, Coach added, "I know we are sad about what happened to Antonio, but we at least won. I'd like to give a shoutout to

Leonard for being a great Assistant Coach who helped lead our team to victory."

Leonard smiled when Coach said that, although I could tell he was pretty disappointed in what had happened to Antonio. "There will be no practice on Monday because it is MLK Day, but on Tuesday, I will talk about the replacement of Antonio," Coach Modella concluded.

"Thank you, Coach," I muttered to Coach Modella before he left.

"Thank you for leading this team at the point guard spot. I know the transition was tough for you, so thanks," Joey Modella responded.

"See you on Tuesday," I added.

"Same with you," he concluded in a grunt.

As I rode in the car heading back home, for some reason, I thought about trying to be friends with Gary. What if he was mean for a reason? Maybe it was time to give my teammate another chance. I knew I had his phone number. Since my phone needed the Internet to text, I would have to wait to come home. Re-living the game helped the 40-minute drive go by pretty quickly, and before I knew it, I was sitting on my bed in my room.

I pulled up the school web page and started looking for the page listing phone numbers. I found the list for sixth graders, and since Gary's last name was Anderson, it was one of the first names on the list. When I finally spotted it, I copied the phone number and pasted it onto where you type the phone number when you want to text somebody. The first text I sent was, "I'm sorry if I have been mean to you. Can we be friends or something? Please get back to me as soon as possible."

I waited all day for a response. I knew that Gary saw it because you could see the three dots that meant he was typing, but then he obviously thought twice because I never received a text.

During dinner, I heard the ding that meant someday texted me. I looked at my phone and saw that Leonard had texted. The text read, "Antonio just told me that his doctor notified him he has a fractured talus, which is a bone in the ankle, and that he is out for the rest of the season."

My mom must have read my expression or the message because she sighed. "I'll clear the dishes tonight if you kids go to sleep right now. I have a surprise for you guys tomorrow!" she exclaimed.

"Can I play basketball for 15 minutes?" I asked.

"Can I play video games for 15 minutes?" Alex questioned.

"Fine, but if you guys are even one second late to bed, you will not get the surprise in the morning, and you will not be able to play video games or basketball for the rest of the week. Do you hear me?" she said with a stern voice.

We both nodded our heads, and Alex sprinted up to his room, and I ran as fast as I could to grab a basketball and my Air Jordan basketball shoes that I hardly ever wore on concrete because they have a chance of getting ruined. But they were very old, and I didn't like them anymore, so I put them on anyway. Since the sun was already set, I went to turn on the lights.

My first shot, a simple free throw, was way too short and barely hit the rim's front side. I had forgotten to bend my knees as much as I should! For the next free throw, I bent my knees a little bit more and hit nothing but net. I shot eight more free throws, and seven of them went in.

After the last shot made the priceless swishing sound, I heard a ring on my phone. It was from Gary. The text read, "You wanna meet on Main Street at 2 p.m. tomorrow?"

I put away the basketball because I had to ask my mom if I could go. As I ran up the stairs, I heard mom crying in her bed. I was guessing it was because of dad. If I were to ask her now, it might make her mad. I decided to risk it and walked right into her room. "Mom, can I go meet someone at 2 p.m. tomorrow?" I asked her.

"Who is it? I would say no if you don't know them," she sobbed.

"Remember when I told you about the guy that kicked Leonard in the shins? I thought it would be a good idea to try to make up with him, and he wants to meet me on Main Street. His name is Gary," I said, hoping her answer would be exactly what I wanted it to be.

"Fine, but only if you let me drive you. Now go to bed," she concluded.

"Thanks. Good night mom," I said as I slowly started to leave the room.

Once I got in my room, I responded to Gary with a thumbs-up emoji, hopeful to start a friendship with him.

I woke up the next morning feeling very tired. It was almost like I hadn't slept the night before. I heard my brother scream, "Oh my gosh! I can't believe it!"

It must have been the surprise mom was talking about. It could not have been that amazing. I put on my favorite Blazers shirt, my gray Nike pants and walked downstairs. I saw a Nike shoebox on our marbled counter. "What is this?" I asked.

"The surprise!" mom exclaimed.

"What did Alex get?" I questioned.

"I got dad's old video game set!" he said.

"Lucky. I probably got a whole box of nothing," I guessed.

I went to the counter where the shoebox was. I opened it up, and I saw them. "Air Jordan 23s! Signed by Michael Jordan! How did dad get these?!" I exclaimed.

My brother sat there with his mouth hanging open. I instantly ran my hand over the signed part of the shoe. The area where Michael Jordan had signed it had a white background, and the bottom part of the shoe was blue. "How did dad get this?" I asked.

"About three years ago, your father told me that if anything were to ever happen to him, to give you those shoes and you that gaming set. That's why I let you guys do what you wanted last night because that's exactly what I got you for the surprise. Now go upstairs and talk to your friends about what you guys just got," she concluded.

Alex did precisely as mom said, but I just sat there, staring at the shoes. "How did he get these in the first place?" I questioned.

"I'll tell you the story on your birthday. Your birthday is only about four weeks from now. The same day as Leonard's birthday!" she exclaimed. "Now, please, go upstairs," she finished.

I did as she said, heading directly to my room. When I entered, I grabbed my phone from my nightstand and took a picture of the shoes. I first sent the picture to a group chat with Leonard, Liam, and Cooper, and then to the chat with everybody on our basketball team who had a phone.

Everybody texted the money emoji and either "Wow!" or "No way!"

For the whole morning, I just sat in bed playing NBA 2K and Madden 22, my two favorite games. Between the combined six games I played between both games against AI, I won four times. Although my brother hardly plays 2K, he's an insane gamer. The games got so intense that I would have forgotten about my meet-up with Gary if he didn't text me 15 minutes in advance saying he was heading over to Main Street now. "Mom, I'm ready to go!" I yelled at her once my 2K game ended.

"Come down here so I can drive you! I would rather start driving from the garage than from your room!" she said.

I laughed, then ran down our brown wooden steps and into the kitchen, where I put on my blue and green Nike shoes. I kind of felt bad for Alex because mom left him home alone.

As we drove down Main Street, I felt Gary wouldn't be there. I stood right where he had told me to be for three minutes, but he never came. Five minutes. Eight minutes. I pulled out my phone to call mom, but she never picked up. I guess that I was going to have to walk home. The worst part was that Gary had lied to me. "I can't believe he would do this to me," I said to myself out loud.

"Do what?" a voice said out of nowhere.

Chapter 9

I turned to my left where I saw Gary, who had spawned out of nowhere. "Where were you? I've been waiting for you!" I questioned, surprised by his arrival.

"Sorry about that. I was just going down to get both of us some ice cream. What kind is your favorite: Vanilla or Cookie Dough?" he said to me with a grin on his face.

"I'll take Vanilla. Why are you being so nice to me all of a sudden?" I added, taking the Vanilla ice cream that he handed to me.

"Well, for starters, you are the first to recognize why I am normally so mean to everybody. I try not to bully others, but I can't help myself. It's almost like a weird habit. I am mad about something. Do not tell anybody I said this, but one day when you were not at school, Leonard and I had an incident. Do not ask for details. Also, my parents divorced when I was only four years old, and I live with my mom. But she works two jobs and I don't get to see her a lot. My dad moved to Missouri. I haven't seen him in a long time."

His saying that made me feel sorry for Gary. Now it all made sense. When he heard that my father had died, he had smiled because Gary finally got to see somebody experience a loss, although I would still think that he would want to help someone get through something similar that he had gone through. Also, in third grade, when we did a project over Mother's Day about how appreciative we are of our mothers, he stormed out of the class crying. Whenever we do a Father's Day card or something that has to do with our family, he would do the same. I suddenly felt so bad for him.

"Can we go on a walk?" he asked me.

"Sure?" I responded, though it came out more like a question.

Throughout the walk, we talked about our experience without having at least one parent to always be there for us.

When we finally returned to where we had begun, he said to me, "Also, one more thing. Let's make a deal: You tell no one about what happened to my family or the incident with Leonard, and you have to call the principal asking to let me back in. You may have to confirm with Leonard's mom to do that, by the way. In return, we become friends just like you said you wanted to be and I am never mean to anybody at school again unless they are being mean to me."

The deal sounded like a good one, but I was not sure if it would work. "This sounds like one of those deals in those FBI shows. But what if the principal says you cannot return to school?" I asked.

"That's fine. I just need you to at least try," he answered.

"In that case, you have yourself a deal," I said while shaking his hand, trying to make it seem like I was a Shark on *Shark Tank*.

We never said anything after that, Gary going down the hill and me going uphill. I was feeling a million times better.

When I finally arrived home, nobody was there. "Mom! Alex! Are you home?!" I yelled.

I heard no response, only the echo of my voice. I started looking around the kitchen. I saw a blue Post-it next to the sink that read, "We had to go grab something at the store. We should be back around 2:45 p.m."

I looked at my FitBit, and the time read 2:39 p.m. When my mom says 2:45 p.m, it usually means around 3:00 p.m. I had 20 minutes to talk to Leonard and his mom about letting Gary return to school. I dialed Leonard's phone number and sat down on our family couch.

He picked up on the third ring, and the first thing he said was, "Why are you calling me on a non-school day?"

"I know. But it's about Gary. I met up with him, and we talked about why he was always so mean to everybody. He is kind of a nice guy. I feel bad for him," I responded.

"Why do you feel bad for him?" he asked.

I had no idea what to do. Leonard was my best friend, and he always had been, but I had made a deal with Gary. "I am not allowed to say," I answered.

"Why not? I am your best friend!" he said in an angry voice.

"I know. I made a deal with him. One part of the deal was I can not tell you why. You can ask him if you want. He even got me ice cream! Don't worry, Leonard; you are still my best friend by a country mile, and you always will be. I will say it to his face if you do not believe me. The main reason why I called is that he wants to go back to school. He said that you and your mom would probably be the only people that can convince the principal that it's okay for him to be back at school. He also told me it is fine if you say no, but as long as I try," I said, trying to sound convincing.

"That is a lot of information you just gave me there. Tell him I say no, only because he kicked me in the shins and ruined my season!" he half-yelled.

"Why are you raging so much?" I asked him.

With that, Leonard hung up on me. I sat on the couch for 15 minutes. How was I supposed to explain this to Gary? Also, since Gary will not be able to go to school, he won't be allowed to attend or play in our game this Thursday. My team probably won't even make it to the playoffs, which had never happened before. One of my problems got solved, but that solved problem formed another problem.

I texted Gary telling him Leonard's reaction. He didn't respond, and when my mom and brother finally came home, Gary still hadn't texted. "How did things go between you two? Why has Gary been bullying you all these years?" my mom asked.

"Things went great! Gary has been mad because he felt like his teacher would always be mean to him in math class!" I lied.

My mom stared at me right in my eyeballs, somehow not flinching. That was the look she gives me when she knows I'm lying. Her mouth opened, but no words came out. It was almost like she was a movie actor put on mute halfway between her part.

She walked away with a grunt, and my brother said, "Someone got mom mad."

Mom heard Alex because she turned around and stared *him* right in the eyes. Her facial expression said it all. Gary still hadn't responded, making me think he was mad. I played basketball for an hour, and I also played a video game that Alex taught me how to play. It was a pretty simple afternoon.

Right before dinner, I did my math homework, which I completely forgot about. Luckily, I only had to go on this website, watch a video, take notes, and post my notes on Google Classroom.

"How has your day been? Give me the best and worst parts," my mom said as she spooned some of the terrible carrot soup she had made for us tonight.

"The best part of my day was getting the video game set, and the worst part was us having to do this," my brother started.

"The best part of my day was getting the Air Jordan's, and the worst part of my day was also having to do this," I joked.

"You guys are so full of it," my mom responded.

When my mom said that, I heard a ding from my phone. It must be from Gary. I looked at it and saw it was from Leonard. The text read, "We r done being friends. U r mean. Did u forget what he did 2 me?"

Chapter 10

Tears started to run down my cheeks. "What's wrong, honey?" my mom asked.

I showed her the text, and she hugged me. Alex had left because he was nowhere to be seen. "I'm sorry, honey," she said, trying to cheer me up. "I'll talk to his mom if you want me to.

I shook my head and ran up to my room. I had a series of flashbacks of Leonard and me having playdates, big grins on our faces. I could hear the sounds of laughter. Then it hit me. Leonard's birthday party was in four weeks. Maybe I wouldn't be invited.

I felt it would be a terrible day when I woke up on Tuesday. "Mom, I don't feel good!" I yelled from my bedroom.

I felt perfectly fine, but I had no intention of going to school that day. "Let me take your temperature!" she responded.

I got very nervous because I knew my temperature was not high or low enough to pass for a cold or fever, so I was in trouble. "I'm coming up right this second with a thermometer!" she continued to yell as she made her way up to my room.

She opened the door to my room and had a cup of tea in her right hand and a thermometer in her left hand. She put the gray thermometer in my mouth, and I just sat there waiting and hoping my temperature would be high. "102.1 degrees. You should stay in bed," she told me.

I couldn't believe I was actually sick. "Go to bed right now. I'll call the school," she concluded.

Laying down in bed, I looked around my room at the basketball posters. After a while, I felt my eyelids start to close. Before I knew it, I had fallen asleep.

When I woke up, the sky was dark. I felt a lot better, which was good. I must have slept all day. I checked my messages, but there were none, which was unusual. "Mom! Are you there?" I yelled.

I heard no response, so I walked into her room. I saw her sleeping in her bed. I checked the time, and it read 9:07 P.M. *I slept for 14 hours? How is that even possible?* I thought.

I didn't feel like playing video games or reading, so I walked into my room and decided to go back to sleep. It was easy to clear my mind out since I had done nothing all day.

I sat in my bed again, listened to *The Dan Patrick Show*, and after probably 45 minutes, I fell asleep.

"Time for school, kids!" I heard my mom yell as I woke up. It was only one more day before we had our basketball game. I would have to continue to see Leonard. This was also our very last game of the regular season. We had climbed into fifth place, and the team ahead of us, the West Linn Saints, were playing against the Portland Timberwolves. We could make the playoffs but needed the Saints to lose and us to win. I liked our chances, given how good the Timberwolves were.

Feeling much better than I had the previous morning, I asked, "What's for breakfast?"

"You will see when you come down! Are you feeling better?" she responded.

"Yep! I'm on my way!" I said.

I put on my blue sweatpants and my black short sleeve shirt. Once I was all dressed, I ran downstairs. "Waffles and bacon!" my mom exclaimed.

Waffles and bacon were my favorite things for breakfast, but it would be hard to smile given my whole friend situation. "I know you aren't going to be happy after what happened between you and Leonard, but this may cheer you up," my mom said.

I tried to smile, but it was pretty hard. "Can I take the waffles and bacon for the road? It's only a few minutes walking!" I said.

"Of course!" she responded.

With that, I grabbed the food in a Ziplock bag and ran off to school.

It was nice to walk in silence, especially as it was a lovely sunny day. "Hello, Erik!" I heard Leonard's mom say.

She obviously had no idea what was happening between Leonard and me. I just simply smiled and waved back as I continued walking to school.

When I saw Leonard, he looked directly away from me. Since we shared a locker, he saw me approach and went to the water fountain as if it was the most natural thing to do when your best friend comes to your locker. That is what it was like all day: Leonard and I encountered each other, and he walked away from me. It was almost like we were playing hide and seek. Even at basketball practice, I nailed an almost half-court shot, and he just nodded and said nothing to Coach or me.

At the end of practice, Coach Modella walked up to me and asked, "Is there something going on between you and Leonard? You guys have been acting a bit strange around each other."

"No," I simply responded.

"Okay then. See you tomorrow at the game! Tip-off is at 3:30 P.M. So arrive 15 minutes early!" he exclaimed.

I did my best to smile, although I knew I had utterly failed.

My mom drove me home, and Alex had dinner all prepared and ready when we arrived. "What have you been up to?" my mom asked him, but in a voice that sounded like she was an FBI agent or something.

"I wanted to do something nice for the whole family, and I thought this may be a good way to do that," Alex responded.

Dinner was eaten in almost 100% silence, except when I choked on the macaroni & cheese Alex had prepared for us.

I checked the internet and saw that the Saints had lost their game, not just by two or three points, but by 26. *All we need to do is win tomorrow, and we are in*, I thought.

"Good night, sweetie!" my mom said as I shuffled into bed.

"Good night, mom," I concluded.

That night, I had a terrible nightmare. It was that Leonard didn't invite me to his awesome birthday party. In the night terror, the next day at school, all of the kids were talking about how fun it was, and they all were even wearing hats they had gotten as party favors. I had a feeling I was not going to be invited.

When I woke up in the morning, I somehow was happy. It was game day! My mom told me that Leonard would not be attending the game and would not be attending school because he had to go to the doctor's office, and after the appointment, he would be tired. "Get dressed! It's time for school!" my mom yelled, as always.

I was already dressed since I was so excited to be able to go back to school without feeling pressured to pretend to be nice to Leonard. I went downstairs, grabbed breakfast, and went out the door. I had grown addicted to doing that routine, even though I had only used it for two days.

The day went by relatively slowly, me looking up at the clock every once in a while, waiting for school to end and my basketball game to begin.

When my final class finally dragged by, which was English, I got so excited. When I heard a pencil drop, I would jump out of my seat, thinking it was the bell. "Class is over, kids! I will see you guys tomorrow!" my teacher, Mrs. Tart, said.

Seconds after that, the bell rang, and I got out of my seat and ran over to my locker. School ended at 3:00 P.M., and I had to be at my game by 3:15 P.M. at the gym that was ten minute from our house, so everything was kind of one-right-after-another. And as our school didn't have a school bus that takes us to games and I needed to drop my things off at home, I had to go to our house before the game.

I grabbed my backpack from my locker and ran out of the building. "Thank you, Mrs. Tart," I said in a rush as I saw my English teacher in the hallway on my way out of the building.

She responded, but I was long gone by then, soaring through the streets on my way home.

When I finally arrived home, I asked, "Mom, how much longer until I can head to the game?"

"We can go right now if you want," my mom said.

"Let's go then!" I concluded.

With my new Air Jordan's on, we got into the Volvo and headed to the game. We were playing the Hood River Panthers, the only other team in our league from Hood River. Being in 9th place in the league, the Panthers didn't have anything on the line as they no longer had a chance of participating in the playoffs that would begin in two days. But we sure had a lot on the line. Survive and advance or lose and go home.

After waiting for about five minutes inside the gym, I finally met Coach Modella at the sidelines. "Are you ready for the game today?" he asked.

"Of course I am, Coach!" I exclaimed.

I went into the shooting lines, and from how we were warming up, our team wasn't playing that well, except for Jack and me. "We need to win today, or we are out of the playoffs," I said nervously to those around me. "But if we win, we're in."

They all nodded, and no words were said, showing they were also nervous. I dribbled around the three point-line and buried a three-ball. I was on fire! Shootarounds can never predict how you play in the game, so I was trying not to get overconfident. "Gather around! I am going to give out the starting five!" Coach Modella exclaimed.

"Our starters are Adam, Bodhi, Noah, Jack, and Erik," Coach Modella said.

I got a little nervous as he called my name last since he typically calls it first. I stepped onto the court, knowing this was a big game for us. I also was relieved that Jack would finally be getting his first start of the season. Luckily, there was only one good player on the Panthers. He was Bodhi's friend from a summer camp named Jake. The ball was tipped, and the game was underway.

Chapter 11

The Panthers wore black and blue outfits, which were kind of funny given that it was a complete copy of the NFL team, the Carolina Panthers. Bodhi won the jump ball, and he passed me the ball immediately. I dribbled up the court and saw Jack make a nice cut around the three-point line. I did a bounce pass, and he received the ball with ease. Jack took a few dribbles inward, trying to make the defender think that he was going in for the layup, but instead, he took a huge step back and pulled up for the three-pointer. He missed it.

Jake got the rebound and passed it to Richard, a player for the Panthers. He passed back to Jake, who dribbled the ball up the court. He did a pump fake around the free throw line, followed by a jumper from the elbow. Nailed it.

Adam inbounded the ball, and he passed the ball to me. I saw Richard coming toward me, so I passed up to Noah. "Ball!" I heard Jack yell when Noah was around half-court. Noah motioned with his free hand to cut under the hoop running left, and Jack found himself wide open for a reverse layup that he made.

The Panthers responded with a three-ball made by Jake and the assist by Richard, strong offense on both sides of the court being on full display. The score was 5-2, with ten minutes of running clock left in the quarter. "This is a good game we are playing here," I heard the Panthers coach say in the huddle. I thought this was their best two minutes of the season. Why did this have to come against us?

When we got the ball back, Adam had a wide-open shot at the three-point line, but he instead passed it, and Ben, a player for the Panthers, intercepted it. "What was that about? I don't care if you're Steph Curry or Adam Greenstein; when you have an open shot, take it!" Coach Modella complained.

Ben passed the ball immediately to Jake, who was at the three-point line, and he nailed the bucket. "It's okay. We'll score the next one. I promise," I said to Noah, who seemed disappointed about how the game was starting.

We did score on the next possession. When I was at the three-point line, I pulled up for the three-ball, and while in the air, I passed it to Bodhi, and he made an easy layup.

All quarter, it was just layup after layup. At least in the Panthers' case. My team couldn't make anything, even if it felt like the defender was a whole universe away. I knew exactly why. I had not attempted to shoot one single bucket. That was about to change. I *had* to flip the switch.

"Come into the huddle, kids!" Coach Modella yelled in urgency.

At the end of the first quarter, the score was 20-4, the Panthers on top, so I understood why he was mad. Our season was on the line, and we were getting crushed by a team with no chance of making it to the playoffs.

"Does anybody know why we are getting crushed?" Coach Modella said in an angry voice.

"Because Erik isn't shooting, and Antonio and Leonard are out injured?" Bodhi guessed.

"Exactly! The only thing we can change about those three things is giving Erik the ball. That is our second quarter strategy. Give Erik the ball!" Coach Modella said in enthusiasm.

I felt bad for the other kids on my team who Coach told not to shoot, but deep inside, I knew that was what needed to happen. I turned in the stands to look for my dad, to see if he knew exactly what was about to happen. And seeing my mom with an empty seat beside her reminded me he was gone. I wanted to start crying and hide in my room until I completely forgot what had happened. But I knew I couldn't do that, not in the middle of maybe the most important game of my life.

Once I stepped foot back on the court, just like always, my head was cleared of everything else happening in my life except basketball. I took a deep breath and mentally flipped a switch. Our first possession was great, where Adam passed it to me at the three-point line, and I shot the ball instantly. Splash!

When Jake inbounded the ball to Richard, Bodhi stole it and shot it out of Coach Modella's orders. Made it. "The Splash Brothers are here!" Bodhi said, basically calling himself Klay Thompson and myself Steph Curry (or vice versa, you never really know what is going through Bodhi's mind).

The Panthers failed to respond, and halfway through the second quarter, the score was tied at 22. The Panthers' only points came when Bodhi fouled Jake on a layup, and he nailed both free throws. Coach made the subs, having Michael, Marcus, David, Sam, and Noah coming off the bench. "We need you guys to play great defense until the quarter ends!" Coach yelled.

They failed to do as Coach asked, giving up 11 points while we only scored three. At the end of the half, the score was 33-25, the

Panthers winning. "We need to win this game! As I always say: Don't get too high and not too low. Now let's get back out there and win this game! Ducks on three!" Coach said in the halftime huddle.

"One, two, three, Ducks!" our team chanted louder than ever in unison.

When we took the court, we knew that we wanted it more than they did and that we would win. The Panthers starters took the court, also knowing they would win. Richard inbounded the ball to Jake, and the second half began.

Chapter 12

Jake dribbled up the court, eyes fixed on Ben, and passed it to him. Bodhi sensed the pass coming, practically standing on top of Ben. Ben tried to pass it back to Jake immediately before Bodhi took it, but he failed, and I stole the ball. "Cut under left!" I yelled at Bodhi.

That was our signal for him to cut left under the hoop. He did exactly as I instructed, but when he caught the ball, it bounced off his knee and slowly rolled out of bounds. "Come on, Bodhi, we can't be throwing away free points like that!" I said, getting a little frustrated myself.

Richard inbounded the ball to Jake, and he slowed down the pace of the game by dribbling up the floor very slowly. He and Richard were playing some sort of hot potato game because they just passed the ball back and forth, all the way to the three-point line. Jake pulled up and missed it. Ben got the rebound, handed it back to Jake, who did a pump fake. He passed the ball back to Ben, standing wide open right under the hoop, and made a simple off-the-backboard shot.

That one was a killer. Even though the game wasn't even near the final buzzer, giving up an offensive rebound that resulted in points in a win-or-go-home game hurt. Jack still managed to make the inbounds pass to me, and I dribbled up the court in urgency. Everybody on the Panthers knew I liked passing the ball more than shooting it, so I decided to keep it for myself and take the layup. Jake had very long arms, so I had to get some height on the layup to make it, and I got it to rattle in. 35-27, Panthers on top.

The Panthers came back up the court, Jake leading the way, while some other players headed to their spots inside the key or around the arc. Jake made a carefree pass to Ben that was way over his head, who somehow caught it, shot it, but missed it.

I secured the rebound, making sure nobody could steal it from me, and I passed it to Adam. As I was the point guard, Adam passed it right back to me. I took the ball upcourt. I scanned the floor, looking for an open teammate. Bodhi and Noah were both open, but since Noah was closer to the hoop, I threw a dart right into his hands, where he caught it, wasted no time in shooting it, and nailed it; the home crowd was not happy about the mini-comeback. "That's what I'm talking about!" Coach Modella exclaimed.

That brought a smile to the whole team, especially Noah, who had been the one to make the praised bucket. The game slowed down a little bit, with nobody scoring for two minutes. Coach made the subs to give the starters a chance to rest for the final quarter. The secondary group did a great job of keeping the game within reach, converting on five of six shots. The Panthers struggled, on the other hand, only making three out of the five shots they took. The score was 43-40 at the end of the third quarter, the Panthers still winning, but by a much smaller margin. "That is what I like to call superb defense! Just keep up the good play!" Coach exclaimed.

"Should we do the Ducks chant or something else?" Bodhi asked.

"I know! Mo-de-lla! Mo-de-lla! Mo-de-lla!" I lead the team in chanting.

The team continued to chant, and Coach must have had the biggest smile in human history. My team got back on the court; all fired up.

I got the inbounds pass from Adam, and the fourth and final quarter was underway. I didn't see anybody open, so I continued dribbling. When I saw Jack cut under the hoop, heading toward the right corner, I passed it to him. He received the ball about two feet in front of the three-point line. He dribbled backward, took the off-balance three-pointer, and nailed the three-ball. "Let's go, Jack!" I yelled, starting to really get into the game.

Ben instantly inbounded the ball to Jake, who took the ball up the court. He dribbled to what was almost the free throw line and passed it to Ben. What Ben didn't see coming was me absolutely Anthony Davis-like rejecting him on the easy layup. Unfortunately, Jake got the rebound and made a mid-range shot off the glass I almost blocked again. I clapped my hands together in frustration, but I knew we still had a good chance of winning.

The Panthers were back in front, 45-43. When we got the ball, I passed the rock to Adam, but the pass was a little off target, and Ben stole the ball. He stopped at the three-point line and looked around himself to see if anybody was around him. Nobody was. He took the shot and made it easily, a little shimmy at the end.

The game slowed down again, with both teams failing to convert on the next two possessions. I got the ball at the half-court line and dribbled up the floor. I saw a perfect opening for Noah or Bodhi to run to, so I did the signal, and Bodhi converted on the reverse layup. "That's what I like to see!" Coach Modella said from the sidelines.

Jake dribbled up the court with urgency, shot the long three-pointer, and it bounced off the rim and into the hands of Ben. He passed it back to Jake, who missed the makeable teardrop shot. Bodhi got the rebound and passed the ball to me. I tried to somewhat dribble out the clock, not wanting to give them time to push the game out of reach but give us enough time to take the lead. I was sweating like crazy, and my heart was beating faster than I could remember. When I finally took the shot from behind the three-point line, with Richard running at full speed at me, I pulled up for three. Even though he didn't get my arm, I sold the foul and fell onto the floor. The ref blew the whistle and said I was fouled and would get three free throws.

I knew how important the free throws were since there was so little time remaining in the game. I made the first one with ease, but the second bounced off the wrong side of the rim. On the final one, I bent my knees a little more than I had for the second one and sank the shot. The score was 48-47, the Panthers winning with three 2:57 remaining, and possibly our season.

Since it was the Panthers' ball, they had the advantage. Jake inbounded the ball to Deandre, a starter for the Panthers, and he dribbled up the court. He passed it to Jake, who took the shot from the three-point line. Nothing but net.

When we got the ball back down by four points, Adam passed the ball to Jack feeling a sense of urgency. Jack immediately passed the rock to a running Bodhi, who nailed the layup. "That's some good passing!" Coach Modella acknowledged from the sidelines.

It was definitely not our best game defensively, but our offense was solid, and we were now only down by two points.

The Panthers came back with the ball, ready to take the game home and spoil our playoff hopes. But we didn't like the sound of that. When Richard passed the ball to Jake, Noah stole the ball. He passed to me, and I calmly dribbled the ball up the court.

Given that Ben was heavily guarding me, I knew that Bodhi had a better shot than me. But just as I was about to flip it to Bodhi, who was a couple of feet to my left, Ben jumped out to my left to try to block the pass, and I decided to take the three-pointer from the very top of the key.

Since a win secured a playoff berth, and we were down by only two points, it was my biggest shot of the season. Nothing but the bottom of the net, and a frown upon all of the Panthers. We took the lead by one.

When they got the ball back, they rushed up the court. When Jake finally had the open look he needed, he took the shot from the three-point line. He missed it off the right side of the rim. They had no chance of getting the rebound since Noah instantly had his hands on the ball. He took his time dribbling, the score being 52-51, our team winning with 1:31 remaining in the game. I could almost smell the victory.

Noah took about 30 seconds dribbling the ball, with no shot clock in our league. When he had the ball right under the hoop, he flung the ball in my direction, and I pulled up for the three. Splash! Clutchest shot of my life. "Way to go, Erik!" Coach said with maybe too much enthusiasm.

Since there was only a minute left in the game, the Panthers felt a rush to score a basket. Jake drove with the ball, took two steps, went in for the layup, missed it, but got fouled in the process by Jack.

The first free throw was nearly an air ball, probably from the nerves and how vital the shot was, just barely skimming the front side of the rim. The second shot didn't look like it was going in either, but it got saved by a lucky bounce off the rim, and the ball landed in the hoop. We were up by three points, and it was our ball with 45 seconds left in the game.

I tried to dribble the game out, but I got fouled and forced to go to the free throw line with 10 seconds remaining in the game. I made the first one with ease, and the crowd was mad at the made shot. "That's what I'm talking about!" Coach Joey Modella exclaimed.

The second one was also made easily, hitting nothing but net. When Ben got the ball at half-court, he took maybe two dribbles and pulled up for the shot. Missed it. I got the rebound, passed it to Bodhi, who had nobody within ten feet of him, and he dribbled the ball out to

the final buzzer. Ball game. "Playoffs, here we come!" Coach exclaimed

when the buzzer sounded.

Chapter 13

"We played a great game today, kids! The Panthers were better than we expected, but we still pulled through for the win, even without a few great players not with us today. Great job, team!" Coach Joey Modella exclaimed.

"Play-offs! Play-offs! Play-offs!" a couple of kids on my team chanted.

"One seeded Portland Timberwolves, here we come!" Adam exclaimed.

"Oh yeah, one more thing I forgot to tell y'all at halftime. The Salem Grizzlies, the three seed, just lost their game, and with our win, that puts *us* as the three seed! So we're going against the Blue Dogs again, who have beaten us, but we'll make sure that doesn't happen again. You kids better rest up because in two days we have the semifinals, and the day after that is the finals, and I sure hope we are playing in the big game," Coach Modella said.

Our whole team celebrated yet again as we all parted in our separate ways. When I finally found my mom, she hugged me so hard it hurt. "I'm so proud of you, Erik!" my mom exclaimed after she saw me. Since Alex was having a playdate with his friend, he didn't have to go to the game. I thanked Coach Modella, and he gave me a friendly pat on the back in appreciation of my effort.

That night, I felt bad for Alex; everybody at dinner talked about my big win. "What should we do to celebrate?" my mom asked as we were clearing the dishes.

Since I felt bad for Alex, I said, "I say we do whatever Alex wants!"

My mom smiled at me, and Alex just simply grinned. "How about Jeremino's Ice Cream!" he exclaimed.

Everybody in town knew that Jeremino's was the best, and by a lot. We all put on our shoes and hopped into the car. We talked about what flavor we would get and what sizes were allowed.

"May we please get one small Chocolate Chip and one small Cookie Dough?" my mom ordered when we finally arrived.

"Of course you may!" the worker at Jeremino's responded.

We ate at the treehouse right next to the chairs and tables my mom sat at. "It's time to go, kids. It's getting dark," my mom said when both of us had finished our ice cream.

We all crammed back into the car, my mom almost losing her purse in the process. "We are going straight to bed when we get home," my mom declared.

"Okay," we both responded.

We did as she said when we arrived, going straight to our rooms. I arrived, took off my shoes, ran up to my bedroom, and went to bed in a matter of minutes.

I woke up the next morning, not hearing any "louder than typical" noises from my mom, which was a big surprise. I put on my school clothes and went downstairs to see my mom making eggs and waffles. "Can you please eat here today, not on your way to school?" my mom pleaded.

"Fine," I shrugged.

I ate breakfast as fast as possible, and my mom didn't even notice when I left without a single crumb on the plate. I walked up to school as slowly as possible, trying to avoid Leonard as much as I could that day, which included at the start of school.

"Hey Erik," Cooper greeted me when I came through the doors to enter the school building.

I waved back, but I didn't pay him much attention. I only had to survive school to avoid Leonard because we didn't have basketball practice that day. The second I saw Leonard leave our locker, I put my belongings in it.

My first class was Math, which Leonard luckily was not in. It was kind of weird to think that each class that Leonard was not I was excited for, given that it had been the opposite since kindergarten, but I couldn't control the fact that he didn't want to be friends with me.

After Math, I had Social Studies, which Leonard was in. Since we were doing reading groups for that class, it was fine since we were in different groups.

Following Social Studies was recess, but that got canceled because of the heavy rain. I played cards with Bodhi and Noah during that time, but we were doing more talking about basketball than we were playing cards.

I only had one more class with Leonard that day, and it was English, which I hated. What is the point of English class when everybody at our school knows how to speak English? I did a pretty good job avoiding him, except when I had to read one page of the book we were reading together. When it came to that, we each did our reading, closed the book, and called it good. I didn't see him for the rest of the school day. Mission accomplished.

It made me sad to think that we were avoiding each other like we were with all of the fantastic memories we had made. But I knew that we would eventually become friends again soon, but it was more of a matter of when we would make up.

"Hey! Guess what? My doctor cleared me to play ball tomorrow! He said I could only play for 10 minutes total, but that's better than nothing!" I heard Leonard say to Bodhi as he left school.

"That's awesome!" Bodhi exclaimed.

I heard them talk for a little longer, but their conversation was pretty boring after a while.

"Bye!" I yelled over to Bodhi as I walked out of the building.

"Yep, see you tomorrow, Erik," Bodhi responded as Leonard stared at the floor, trying to avoid all eye contact with me.

I took my time on my way home, not in a rush to get to a basketball game. I only had one, and hopefully two, games left in the season, and no school in between!

When I arrived at my house, I took off my school shoes and put on my old Air Jordan basketball shoes. I went back outside and started shooting baskets. I had asked if Bodhi could come over, but he was supposedly getting a haircut. I started nailing bucket after bucket, hardly missing one single shot. I did that for about an hour. I primarily focused on free throws, and became very consistent with the shot, knowing that free throws were one of the most important parts of basketball.

When I finally went back inside, it was almost time for dinner, so I decided to finish my science homework. When I finally finished it, I set the dinner table, knowing how much my mom hated to set the table. "Thank you, honey," she said when she saw me setting the table.

"You're welcome," I responded, pride filled within me.

"You better eat well because the game is at 8:00 A.M., and you have to arrive at 7:45," she warned. "At the least, the game is here in Hood River," she continued. Once everyone was seated, my mom asked, "How was school today, Alex?"

"It was fine. The worst part was that we had to write something about our fathers, and I just told the teacher that I needed to go to the restroom," he responded.

Mom hugged him, both of them experiencing the pain together. We didn't talk much for the rest of dinner. Because of dad.

My mom came in before I went to bed to tuck me in. "I'm sorry about what happened at dinner, honey," she said.

"It's not your fault," I responded.

She squeezed my cheek, and I didn't complain at all, which I usually do, because I knew that my mom was dealing with a lot right now, and I didn't want to make her feel not loved. "Good night," I concluded.

The next morning, I woke up to my mom. It was game day! "Hurry up; you're going to be late for your game," she said.

I put on the blue team jersey that I always wore. When I was finally downstairs, I saw that there was no breakfast. The time was 6:45 A.M. I ran to the door and yelled at my mom to get in the car.

When I finally arrived at the gym, I saw a few kids on my team in layup lines, so I joined them. I heard my phone buzz, and it was Gary telling me that he would be able to go on the court after the game. I smiled because it felt like forever since I had seen him last. "Erik, ball!" Jack yelled towards me when his ball rolled over to where I was sitting on the bench.

I passed it back to him, and he nailed a reverse layup with his right hand. We did a few more drills, all of which Coach oversaw us doing. He commented on my shoes, something he hadn't done last game. "Thank you," I politely responded.

When I saw Leonard enter the building, I got nervous. He went to Bodhi and talked with him until Coach called us in. I was a little jealous that Bodhi was his new best friend instead of me, but I decided it was better to use the anger as drive when I was on the court.

"Leonard, I will only put you in if it is necessary, so don't expect to be a starter. He gave out positions, which were the same as the last game. The Blue Dogs' starting five was Frederick, Shawn, John, Isaac, and Jacob. The referee blew his whistle, the ball was tipped, and the playoff game was underway.

Chapter 14

The Dogs won the jump ball, which was expected given that our team had lost some length with Antonio's injury. The Blue Dogs were one of two teams that only lost one game all season. Frederick started dribbling until he found Isaac cut under the hoop, and he passed it to him. He received the ball mid-step, and he made the reverse layup.

When we got the ball back, I passed the ball to Bodhi immediately. He didn't waste any time passing to Jack, standing alone at the three-point line. Splash!

The Dogs took their time to dribble up the court, obviously not feeling any pressure. Frederick got the ball and made a simple layup, scaring away Adam, who was in his path. The Blue Dogs' did that same play on their next four positions, and Frederick didn't miss once. We were also productive on those four possessions, scoring 11 points on those possessions, all of which were scored by Jack and me. We were a great 1-2 punch in three-point shooting. The Dogs took a timeout with eight minutes left in the opening quarter, the score being 14-10, our team winning. The game was filled with poor defense. We got the ball back when the timeout was over, and no substitutions were made.

Adam inbounded the ball to me, and I took a few dribbles before I passed the ball to Jack. He pulled up for the three but missed it off the right side of the rim where it meets the backboard. Luckily, Noah was right under the hoop for the rebound, and he converted on the layup over Isaac. The Dogs responded with a layup made by Frederick off of an impressive no-looker behind-the-back pass by Isaac.

That's when my team went on a run. I started to nail three-pointer after three-pointer, making every one of the seven shots I took with ease. I was on a roll. I had never made seven three-pointers in one game, let alone all in a row. "That's what I'm talking about!" Coach Modella exclaimed with pride.

Bodhi couldn't help himself but say, "Send this kid to the NBA already!"

My team's defense was the best it had been all season. Up to that point in the game, we just wanted to win the game more than the Dogs did, giving up only two points during this stretch, the shot being made by Frederick when he was wide open at the elbow. The score was 37-14, our team up with two minutes left in the opening quarter. Coach decided to put Leonard in the game. With me. That could go badly.

When Adam inbounded the ball to me, I started to dribble to the left, not seeing many people open. Except for Leonard. I passed it to him, and he smiled when the ball was into his hands and pulled up for the three-pointer. Nothing but net. "He is baaaack!" Coach exclaimed with a huge grin on his face.

Leonard didn't thank the passer, which happened to be me, which Coach had always pushed us to do. The Dogs responded with a layup made by Jacob. Nobody made a basket for the rest of the quarter,

Leonard missing both of his shots. "We are winning 40-16! This is crazy!" Bodhi exclaimed, filled with enthusiasm.

"At this rate, we are going to score 160 points!" Leonard added.

Coach took out all of the starters and put in the backups. The Dogs left some of their starters in, and others out.

When the second quarter resumed, I had a feeling it would be a quarter of defense. The Dogs' first possession was a great play. Shawn inbounded the ball to a player named Miles, who dribbled all the way to the three-point line. He flung the ball right under the hoop where Shawn received the ball and hit one of the greatest shots I had ever seen when he caught the ball and shot instantaneously while in midair. We responded when Sam shot from the three-point line, missed, but got fouled. He made two of the three free throws.

The Dogs failed to respond when Frederick got blocked on a layup by Sam. Sam got the rebound, passed to Lukas, and he slowed the game down. Lukas dribbled to the half-court line and passed it to Sam, who tried to make the mid-range bucket but missed it, giving the Dogs the ball back.

It went back and forth, neither team being able to take advantage of open shots, except for when Sam nailed a reverse layup, as well as when Frederick converted on the fadeaway three-ball. It was just solid defense on both sides of the ball, for at least nine minutes of the game, leaving just under one minute left in the half.

The Dogs got the ball, inbounded it to Isaac, and he took off dribbling. He went all the way to the free throw line. Noah was guarding him, and yelled, "Brick!" as loud as he could when he shot it, but it didn't phase Isaac one bit as he banked it off the backboard into the basket.

When Sam got the ball back, he tried to make a fadeaway three-ball, but he missed off the left side of the rim. The Dogs got the rebound, but Frederick made a lazy pass to Jacob and didn't see Sam coming in to steal it. He took one dribble, did a pump fake on Jacob, and nailed the shot off the glass. There were only three seconds left, so all the Dogs could do was throw the ball as far as they could, which wasn't even close to the hoop. "We are winning 46-23! We are almost guaranteed to go to the finals!" Noah exclaimed.

"Don't get too overconfident; there is still a whole half of ball to be played. If you guys can go up 46-23 in a half, then they are more than capable of doing the same," Coach Modella warned. We all nodded and then we huddled up as a group. "We are playing some really good ball out there, but as I told Noah, don't get overconfident, or they will go on a run. Now, go get some water. Secondary group, you will be going out for all of the third quarter, no matter what happens. Leonard, I'll put you in for the end of the next two quarters," Coach said.

We all drank some water, did a little bit of stretching, and the secondary group got out onto the court. "We just need good defense!" Coach Modella reminded the players.

The second half started fine, with both teams making layups on the first possession. It was their ball, and Frederick was the inbounder. He passed it to Isaac, who was at the half-court line. He dribbled once to his left, passed back to Frederick, who had a relatively quiet first half, and swished a three from the top of the key.

When we got the ball back, we failed to respond, Michael missing on a contested deep three-ball that he probably should not have taken. The Dogs got the ball back, Shawn throwing a bullet to the three-point line where Frederick was, and he did a pump fake, went in for the layup, and nailed it. On our next possession, we couldn't get anything when Lukas missed a layup that I had seen him make way more times than I had seen him miss.

It went like that for a while, Frederick and Shawn making shots non-stop off the assists from Isaac and John. Our defense was playing poorly, and our offense was even worse. We made zero shots, and the Dogs were going on the run I had feared they were capable of. "I asked you guys to do one thing! You need to focus on playing defense. Guard your man! Help your teammates!" Coach complained, full of anger.

It went on like that for seven minutes; everybody in the bleachers was happy, and my helplessness on the bench made me feel even worse. By the time Leonard came in, the score was 50-48, the Beaverton Blue Dogs now in the lead.

"I told you that the Dogs were going to go on a run!" Coach yelled, frustrated at seeing his finals hopes falling apart in a matter of 15 minutes. "Leonard! You are in!" Coach yelled.

Leonard high-fived David, the one who he was subbing in for. The inbound pass went to him. He took the ball for a few seconds and passed it to Lukas, who went in for the layup. Lukas missed it, but he got his own rebound and passed it to Leonard at the free throw line. Swish!

"One more minute!" I yelled from the sidelines.

My whole team rushed back on defense, but it was too late. Shawn threw the ball as far as he could the length of the court, and it landed right in the hands of John, standing right under the hoop, waiting for the play to happen. "Make this the last play!" Coach ordered from the sidelines after John got it to go off the glass.

Our team did precisely as Coach pleaded, taking our time dribbling up the court. Leonard pulled up for the three when there were just four seconds left. Nothing but net.

The Dogs called a timeout, giving them the ball at half-court. When they inbounded it, they only had two seconds. Frederick got the ball and passed it to Isaac, who made the layup right as the buzzer sounded. The score was 53-52; we were winning with one quarter remaining. "We need to play better defense! Giving up last-second points like that is unacceptable!" Coach said.

"We weren't doing well offensively either," Sam pointed out.

"Luckily, we have one more quarter left to play, and I know you guys will win! If you bend your knees and follow through, we are unbeatable! Now let's go finish this game off strong!" Coach exclaimed.

Chapter 15

We all cheered, and the starters, including myself, got back onto the court. All of the starters for the Dogs were also playing. We got the ball to start the final quarter, and it began with Adam inbounding the ball to Noah. He took a few dribbles, handed it off to me, and I threw a rocket to Bodhi, who made a layup in transition.

The Blue Dogs moved quickly, wasting no time passing the ball. The play ended with a three-ball by Frederick that was drilled. It went like that for a good while, Jack or I making a shot, and then Frederick making a three-ball or a layup. With five minutes left in the game, Coach put Leonard in. "Leonard! Get in the game! I need you to keep on shooting!" He had exclaimed, pointing at his jersey.

He was going in for Bodhi, who wasn't playing his strongest game. It was the Dogs' ball, so Leonard had to play defense. He was relatively tall with long arms, so when John went up for the layup, he got rejected by Leonard, who barely had to jump. Miraculously, he passed to me, and I sent the rock over to Noah, who nailed the layup. This time up the court, the Dogs took their time with the ball, and Frederick sank the three-point shot, Jack stepping backward and giving him space. The score was now 76-70, the Blue Dogs winning with only three minutes remaining.

"Come on, guys! This is our season on the line!" Coach yelled.

It was our ball, and I was the inbounder. I sent the rock to Leonard, who dribbled the ball up the court. When he reached just past half-court, he faked the pass to Noah, took two more dribbles up the court, and banked in the three-ball from range. Three-point game. The Dogs took their time, trying to eat the clock, so we didn't have time to make a comeback. When Frederick finally pulled up for the two-point shot, he got nervous, and the ball bounced off the rim and into the hands of Leonard. He passed the ball to me.

Although we didn't talk about it, I think Leonard kind of wanted to be friends with me again, but I didn't know why. I knew that passing someone a basketball isn't the #1 sign of friendship, but that was an improvement from a few days ago. I got the ball, sent it to Noah, and he tried to make the layup. He missed it. "Tweet! Foul! Two shots!" the referee yelled from the spot of the foul.

As always, the person who was guilty of the foul complained to the ref, but that debate didn't go his way, and Noah still got two shots. You could tell Noah was super nervous with so much on the line, and on the first shot, he got a lucky bounce off the rim and into the hoop. "There we go, Noah!" Coach cheered.

For the second shot, the ball looked like it was going to hit the rim again, but it instead hit nothing but net. Now the Blue Dogs were only up by one point. Again, they took their time dribbling up the court. John shot the three-pointer, and it hit the rim and fell into the hands of Shawn. He whipped the ball over to Frederick, who pulled up for the three-ball.

As always, he swished it. Forty-one seconds left in the game, and possibly our season.

It was our ball, down by four and we had to move quickly. "We don't need a three-pointer!" Coach yelled while pacing the sidelines.

Adam inbounded the ball to me, and I raced up the court. I scanned the floor for open players, but nobody was open. I started to run faster. Still, nobody was open. Almost to the hoop, I jump-stopped and took the mid-range jumper. Nailed it.

Twenty-three seconds left in the game, Blue Dogs up by two. Frederick got the ball and tried to take his time, but the defenders for my team were swarming him like bees. He was forced to pass the ball to Isaac, who was the only person who was open. He looked around for open teamates, but there weren't any. Twelve seconds. Isaac looked behind him, and before he could do anything with the rock I came in and swiped the ball out of his hands.

I went up the court as fast as possible, seeing I would have to be the one to make either the tying or game-winning basket. Isaac was faster than I expected, and with five seconds left in the game, he fouled me. Since it wasn't a shooting foul, I wouldn't get free throws, but it would be our ball at half-court. "We need to draw up a play!"

Coach's plan was simple: Give me the rock at the three-point line, let me take a couple dribbles to my left and pull up for the win. I knew I would make the shot if I had the chance.

Adam was the inbounder, and when the referee blew his whistle, he passed it to me; no defenders there to steal it like in the game against the Timberwolves. Three seconds. I was getting crammed between two defenders, meaning somebody had to be open. It was Leonard. Two seconds. For the slightest moment, everything around me froze as I heard a voice in my head. It was my father's voice. "Friendship is the most important thing in life," I heard my dad say inside my head.

I had a flashback to when I was at a park with him when I was eight years old, throwing around a football. We were talking about an argument I was in with my friend Charlie. I was asking him how I should resolve the fight or if I should just stop being friends with him altogether. And that is exactly what he had told me: friendship is the most important thing in life.

As I was brought back into the present, I heard the bottom of a shoe make that squeaking sound against the court. There were two seconds on the game clock. Remembering that Leonard was the man open, I threw the ball over one of the defender's waving arms. One second left. He caught the ball and instantly pulled up for the three from the left wing to send us to the finals. Everything became quiet. The ball soared through the air. I could see the grin on Leonard's face. It was going in. I knew it was going in. Boink! Boink!

The ball bounced off of the left side of the rim twice. *Come on, please go in*, I thought. As the ball bounced up again, I knew it wouldn't go in. I couldn't even watch. When I opened my eyes, I saw the ball still bouncing on the floor and the Beaverton Blue Dogs storming the court, making me want to cry.

I saw Gary come down to where Leonard was. I also decided to walk over there. Leonard just sat there, motionless. "Bro, it's okay. We always have next year. Plus, that was a tough shot, and I could have made a better pass to you," I said to Leonard. He didn't even flinch, frozen in place. And then an idea flashed in my mind. "Hey! Can we be friends? All of us?" I asked, pointing at Gary, then Leonard, and finally myself.

Leonard and Gary sat there, thinking about the question. It felt like forever, watching them think about the question. "Sure," all of us said in unison, smiling.

Although we lost in the semifinals, that is exactly how I wanted my season to end. Just like my dad had said that one day at the park, friendship is the most important thing in life.